DOVER CHILDREN'S THRIFT CLASSICS

Huckleberry Finn

MARK TWAIN

Adapted by Bob Blaisdell

Illustrated by John Green

DOVER PUBLICATIONS
Garden City, New York

DOVER CHILDREN'S THRIFT CLASSICS

EDITOR OF THIS VOLUME: JILL JARNOW

Copyright

Bibliographical Note

This Dover edition, first published in 1999, is a new abridgement of *Adventures of Huckleberry Finn* (first publication in America: Charles L. Webster and Company, New York, 1885). The note and illustrations have been specially prepared for the present edition.

Library of Congress Cataloging-in-Publication Data

Twain, Mark, 1835–1910.
Adventures of Huckleberry Finn / Mark Twain ; adapted by Bob Blaisdell ; illustrated by John Green.
p. cm. — (Dover children's thrift classics)
"This Dover edition, first published in 1999, is a new abridgement of Adventures of Huckleberry Finn . . ."—T.p. verso.
Summary: Recounts the adventures of a young boy and an escaped slave as they travel down the Mississippi River on a raft.
ISBN-13: 978-0-486-40349-6
ISBN-10: 0-486-40349-1
[1. Mississippi River—Fiction. 2. Missouri—Fiction.] I. Blaisdell, Robert. II. Green, John, 1948– ill. III. Title. IV. Series.
PZ7.C584Ab 1999 98-8060
CIP
AC

Manufactured in the United States of America
40349115 2021
www.doverpublications.com

Note

Huckleberry Finn is set along the Mississippi River Valley in approximately 1850. The story revolves around young Huck, traveling by raft with Jim, an escaped slave, who he has promised to help gain his freedom. As the two survive by their wits, and just plain luck, Huck observes what is good and what is bad about his world.

Mark Twain notes at the beginning of the original novel that he has carefully re-created authentic southern speaking styles in the speeches of his characters. For example, Huck narrates the tale in his own "Pike - County" accent. Jim speaks in the style of a black slave living in Missouri. Some characters speak in dialects which are similar, but not identical, to Huck's. Young readers may find that by reading aloud some of the dialogue, they will better understand and enjoy the high adventure and unforgettable characters in this classic story.

*She put me in them new clothes again,
and I couldn't do nothing but feel all cramped up.*

Chapter 1

You don't know about me, without you have read a book by the name of "The Adventures of Tom Sawyer." Now the way that book winds up is this: Tom and me found the money that the robbers hid in the cave, and it made us rich. We got six thousand dollars apiece—all gold. Well, Judge Thatcher, he took it and put it out at interest, and it fetched us a dollar a day apiece, all the year round—more than a body could tell what to do with. The Widow Douglas, she took me for her son, and allowed she would civilize me; but it was rough living in the house all the time, considering how decent the widow was in all her ways; and so when I couldn't stand it no longer, I lit out. I got into my old rags, and was free and satisfied. But Tom Sawyer, he hunted me up and said he was going to start a band of robbers, and I might join if I would go back to the widow and be respectable. So I went back.

The widow she cried over me, and called me a poor lost lamb. She put me in them new clothes again, and I couldn't do nothing but feel all cramped up. Pretty soon I wanted to smoke, and asked the widow to let me. But she wouldn't. She said it was a mean practice.

Her sister, Miss Watson, a tolerable old woman, with goggles on, had just come to live with her, and took a set at me now, with a spelling book. She worked me middling hard for about an hour, and then the widow made her ease up. I couldn't stood it much longer. By-and-by they fetched the slaves in and had prayers, and then everybody was off to bed. I went up to my room, and got out my pipe for a smoke, for the house was all as still as death, now, and so the widow wouldn't know. Well, after a long time I heard the clock away off in the town go boom, boom, boom—twelve licks—and all still again—stiller than ever. Pretty soon I heard a twig snap. I could just barely hear a "me-yow! me-yow!" down in the dark amongst the trees. Says I, "me-yow! me-yow!" as soft as I could, and then I put out the light and scrambled out of the window onto the shed. Then I slipped down to the ground and crawled in amongst the trees, and sure enough there was Tom Sawyer waiting for me.

We went tip-toeing along a path amongst the trees back towards the end of the widow's garden, stooping down so as the branches wouldn't scrape our heads. When we was passing by the kitchen I fell over a tree root and made a noise. We scrounched down and laid still. Miss Watson's big slave, named Jim, was setting in the kitchen door; we could see him pretty clear. He got up and stretched his neck out, listening. Then he says, "Who dah?"

As soon as we heard him go back to sleep, we cut along the path, around the garden house, and by-and-by fetched up on the steep top of the other side of the house. Well, when Tom and me got to the edge of the hill-top, we looked away down into the village and could see three or four lights twinkling; and the stars over us was sparkling ever so fine; and down by the village was the river, a whole mile broad, and awful still and grand. We went down the hill and found Jo Harper

Well, when Tom and me got to the edge of the hill-top, we looked away down into the village and could see three or four lights twinkling.

and Ben Rogers, and two or three more of the boys, hid in the old tanyard. So we unhitched a skiff and pulled down the river two mile and a half, to the big scar on the hillside, and went ashore.

We went to a clump of bushes, and Tom made everybody swear to keep the secret, and then showed them a hole in the hill, right in the thickest part of the bushes. Then we lit the candles and crawled in on our hands and knees. We went about two hundred yards, and then

the cave opened up. Tom poked about among the passages and pretty soon ducked under a wall where you wouldn't a noticed there was a hole. We went along a narrow place and got into a kind of room, all damp and sweaty and cold, and there we stopped. Tom says: "Now we'll start this band of robbers and call it Tom Sawyer's Gang. Everybody that wants to join has got to take an oath, and write his name in blood."

Everybody was willing. Tom made a real beautiful oath, and we asked Tom if he got it out of his own head. He said some of it, but the rest was got out of pirate books, and robber books, and every gang that was high-toned had it.

Then they all stuck a pin in their fingers to get blood to sign with, and I made my mark on the paper. Tom said we would all go home and meet next week and rob somebody and kill some people.

Ben Rogers said he couldn't get out much, only Sundays, and so he wanted to begin next Sunday; but all the boys said it would be wicked to do it on Sunday, and that settled the thing. They agreed to get together and fix a day as soon as they could, and then we elected Tom Sawyer first captain and Jo Harper second captain of the Gang, and so started home.

I clumb up the shed and crept into my window just before day was breaking. My new clothes was all greased up and clayey, and I was dog-tired.

We played robber now and then about a month, and then I resigned. All the boys did. We hadn't robbed nobody, we hadn't killed any people, but only just pretended. We used to hop out of the woods and go charging down on hog-drovers and women in carts taking garden stuff to market. Tom Sawyer called the hogs "gold ingots," and he called the turnips and stuff "jewelry" and we would go to the cave and pow-wow over

what we had done and how many people we had killed and marked. But I couldn't see no profit in it.

Well, three or four months run along, and it was well into the winter, now. I had been to school most all the time, and could spell, and read, and write just a little, and could say the multiplication table up to six times seven is thirty-five, and I don't reckon I could ever get any further than that if I was to live forever. I don't take no stock in mathematics, anyway.

At first I hated the school, but by-and-by I got so I could stand it. I was getting sort of used to the widow's ways, too, and they warn't so raspy on me. Living in a house, and sleeping in a bed, pulled on me pretty tight, mostly, but before the cold weather I used to slide out and sleep in the woods, sometimes, and so that was a rest to me. I liked the old ways best, but I was getting so I liked the new ones, too, a little bit. The widow said I was coming along slow but sure, and doing very satisfactory. She said she warn't ashamed of me.

One morning I went down the front garden and clumb over the stile, where you go through the high board fence. There was an inch of new snow on the ground, and I seen somebody's tracks. I stooped down to look at them. I didn't notice anything at first, but next I did. There was a cross in the left boot-heel made with big nails, to keep off the devil. I knowed it had to be my father.

Pap he hadn't been seen for more than a year, and that was comfortable for me; I didn't want to see him no more. He used to always whale me when he was sober and could get his hands on me; though I used to take to the woods most of the time when he was around. I had judged the old man would turn up again by-and-by, though I wished he wouldn't.

Seeing his footprint I was up in a second and running

down the hill. I looked over my shoulder now and then, but I didn't see nobody. I was at Judge Thatcher's as quick as I could get there. He said, "Why, my boy, you are all out of breath. Did you come for your interest?"

"No, sir," I says; "is there some for me?"

"Oh, yes, a half-yearly is in, last night. Over a hundred and fifty dollars. Quite a fortune for you. You better let me invest it along with your six thousand, because if you take it you'll spend it."

"No, sir," I says, "I don't want to spend it. I don't want it at all—nor the six thousand, nuther. I want you to take it; I want to give it to you—the six thousand and all."

He looked surprised. "Why, what can you mean, my boy?"

I says, "Don't you ask me no questions about it, please. You'll take it—won't you?"

"Is something the matter?"

"Please take it," says I, "and don't ask me nothing—then I won't tell no lies."

"Oho-o. I think I see. You want to *sell* all your property to me—not give it. *That's* the correct idea." He wrote something on a paper and says: "There—you see it says 'for a consideration.' That means I have bought it of you and paid you for it. Here's a dollar for you. Now, you sign it."

So I signed it, and left.

Chapter 2

When I lit my candle and went up to my room that night, there set Pap, his own self!

I had shut the door to. Then I turned around, and there he was. Pap was most fifty, and he looked it. His hair was long and tangled and greasy, and hung down, and you could see his eyes shining through like he was behind vines. It was all black, no gray; so was his long, mixed-up whiskers. There warn't no color in his face, where his face showed; it was white; not like another man's white, but a white to make a body sick, a white to make a body's flesh crawl—a tree-toad white, a fish-belly white. As for his clothes—just rags, that was all. He had one ankle resting on 'tother knee; the boot on that foot was busted, and two of his toes stuck through, and he worked them now and then. His hat was laying on the floor; an old black slouch with the top caved in, like a lid.

I stood a-looking at him; he set there a-looking at me, with his chair tilted back a little. I set the candle down. I noticed the window was up; so he had clumb in by the shed. He kept a-looking me all over. By-and-by he says: "Starchy clothes—very. You think you're a good deal of a big-bug, *don't* you?"

"Maybe I am, maybe I ain't," I says.

Pap was most fifty, and he looked it.

"Don't you give me none o' your lip," says he. "You've put on considerable many frills since I been away. I'll take you down a peg before I get done with you. You're educated, too, they say; can read and write. You think you're better'n your father, now, don't you, because he can't? I'll take it out of you. Who told you you might meddle with such hifalutin' foolishness, hey?—who told you you could?"

"The widow. She told me."

"The widow, hey?—and who told the widow she could put in her shovel about a thing that ain't none of her business?"

"Nobody ever told her."

"Well, I'll learn her how to meddle. And looky here—you drop that school, you hear? I'll learn people to bring up a boy to put on airs over his own father and let on to be better'n what *he* is. You don't lemme catch you fooling around that school again, you hear? Your mother couldn't read, and she couldn't write, nurther, before she died. None of the family couldn't, before *they* died. *I* can't; and here you're a-swelling yourself up like this. I ain't the man to stand it—you hear? Say—lemme hear you read."

I took up a book and begun something about George Washington. When I'd read about a half a minute, he fetched the book a whack with his hand and knocked it across the house. He says: "It's so. You can do it. I had my doubts when you told me. Now looky here; you stop that putting on frills. I won't have it. I'll lay for you, my smarty; and if I catch you about that school I'll tan you good. First you know you'll get religion, too. I never see such a son. Why there ain't no end to your airs—they say you're rich. Hey?—how's that?"

"They lie—that's how."

"Looky here—mind how you talk to me; I'm a-standing about all I can stand, now—so don't gimme no sass. I've been in town two days, and I hain't heard nothing but about you bein' rich. I heard about it away down the river, too. That's why I come. You git me that money tomorrow—I want it."

"I hain't got no money."

"It's a lie. Judge Thatcher's got it. You git it. I want it."

"I hain't got no money, I tell you. You ask Judge Thatcher; he'll tell you the same."

"All right. I'll ask him. Say—how much you got in your pocket? I want it."

"I hain't got only a dollar, and I want that to—"

"It don't make no difference what you want it for—you just shell it out."

He took it, and then he said he was going down town to get some whisky.

Next day he was drunk, and he went to Judge Thatcher's and bullyragged him and tried to make him give up the money, but he couldn't, and then he swore he'd make the law force him. Pap said he'd cowhide me till I was black and blue if I didn't raise some money for him. He went for Judge Thatcher in the courts to make him give up that money, and he went for me, too, for not stopping school. He catched me a couple of times and thrashed me, but I went to school just the same, and dodged him or out-run him most of the time. I didn't want to go to school much, before, but I reckoned I'd go now to spite Pap. That law trial was a slow business; appeared like that warn't ever going to get started on it; so every now and then I'd borrow two or three dollars off the judge for him, to keep from getting a cowhiding. Every time Pap got money he got drunk; and every time he got drunk he raised Cain around town; and every time he raised Cain he got jailed.

He watched out for me one day in the spring, and catched me, and took me up the river about three mile, in a skiff, and crossed over to the Illinois shore where it was woody and there warn't no houses but an old log hut in a place where the timber was so thick you couldn't find it if you didn't know where it was.

He kept me with him all the time, and I never got a

chance to run off. We lived in that old cabin, and he always locked the door and put the key under his head, nights. He had a gun which he had stole, I reckon, and we fished and hunted, and that was what we lived on. Every little while he locked me in and went down to the store, three miles, to the ferry, and traded fish and game for whisky and fetched it home and got drunk and had a good time, and whipped me. The widow she found out where I was, by-and-by, and sent a man over to try to get hold of me, but Pap drove him off with the gun, and it warn't long after that till I was used to being where I was, and liked it, all but the cowhide part.

It was kind of lazy and jolly, laying off comfortable all day, smoking and fishing, and no books nor study. Two months or more run along, and my clothes got to be all rags and dirt, and I didn't see how I'd ever got to like it so well at the widow's, where you had to wash, and eat on a plate, and comb up, and go to bed and get up regular, and be forever bothering over a book and have old Miss Watson pecking at you all the time. I didn't want to go back no more. I had stopped cussing, because the widow didn't like it; but now I took to it again because Pap hadn't no objections. It was pretty good times up in the woods there, take it all around.

But by-and-by Pap got too handy with his beatings, and I couldn't stand it. Once he locked me in and was gone three days. It was dreadful lonesome. I made up my mind I would fix up some way to leave there. I found something at last, an old rusty saw without any handle. I greased it up and went to work. There was an old horse-blanket nailed against the logs at the far end of the cabin behind the table, to keep the wind from blowing through the chinks and putting the candle out. I got under the table and raised the blanket and went to

work to saw a section of the big bottom log out, big enough to let me through. Well, it was a good long job, but I was getting towards the end of it when I heard Pap's gun in the woods. I got rid of the signs of my work, and dropped the blanket and hid my saw, and pretty soon Pap come in.

Pap warn't in a good humor—so he was his natural self. He said he was down to town, and everything was going wrong. His lawyer said he reckoned he would win his lawsuit and get the money, if they ever got started on the trial; but then there was ways to put it off a long time, and Judge Thatcher knowed how to do it. Then the old man got to cussing, and cussed everything and everybody he could think of.

He made me go to the rowboat and fetch the things he had got. There was a fifty-pound sack of corn meal, a side of bacon and a four-gallon jug of whisky. I brought up a load, and went back and set down on the bow of the boat to rest. I thought it all over, and I reckoned I would walk off with the gun and some fishing-lines, and take to the woods when I run away. I guessed I wouldn't stay in one place, but just tramp right across the country, mostly night times, and hunt and fish to keep alive, and get so far away that the old man nor the widow couldn't ever find me any more. I judged I would saw out and leave that night if Pap got drunk enough, and I reckoned he would.

By-and-by I got the things all up to the cabin, and then it was about dark. While I was cooking supper the old man took a swig or two and got sort of warmed up, and went to ripping again. He had been drunk over in town, and laid in the gutter all night, and he was a sight to look at. After supper Pap took the whisky jug. I judged he would be blind drunk in about an hour, and then I would steal the key, or saw myself out. He drank

I brought up a load, and went back and set down on the bow of the boat to rest.

and drank, and tumbled down on the blankets, by-and-by; but luck didn't run my way. He groaned and moaned, and thrashed around this way and that, for a long time. At last I got so sleepy I couldn't keep my eyes open, and so before I knowed what I was about I was sound asleep.

I don't know how long I was asleep, but all of a sudden there was an awful scream, and I was up. There was Pap, looking wild and skipping around every which way and yelling about snakes. He said they was crawling up his legs; then he would give a jump and scream, and say one had bit him on the cheek—but I couldn't see no

snakes. He started and run round and round the cabin, hollering, "Take him off! Take him off! He's biting me on the neck!" I never see a man look so wild in the eyes. Pretty soon he was all tuckered out, and fell down panting; then he rolled over and over, wonderful fast, kicking things every which way, and striking and grabbing at the air with his hands, and screaming, and saying there was devils ahold of him. He wore out, by-and-by, and laid still a while, moaning. Then he laid stiller, and didn't make a sound.

By-and-by he rolled out and jumped up on his feet looking wild, and he see me and went for me. He chased me round and round the place with a clasp-knife, calling me the Angel of Death and saying he would kill me and then I couldn't come for him no more. I begged, and told him I was only Huck, but he laughed such a screechy laugh, and roared and cussed, and kept on chasing me up. Pretty soon he was all tired out, and dropped down with his back against the door, and said he would rest a minute and then kill me. He put his knife under him, and said he would sleep and get strong, and then he would see who was who.

So he dozed off, pretty soon. I got the old split-bottom chair and clumb up, as easy as I could, not to make any noise, and got down the gun. I slipped the ramrod down it to make sure it was loaded, and then I laid it across the turnip barrel, pointing towards Pap, and set down behind it to wait for him to stir. And how slow and still the time did drag on.

"Git up! What you 'bout?"

I opened my eyes and looked around, trying to make out where I was. It was after sun-up, and I had been sound asleep. Pap was standing over me, looking sour—and sick, too. He says, "What you doin' with this gun?"

I judged he didn't know nothing about what he had been doing, so I says: "Somebody tried to get in, so I was laying for him."

"Why didn't you roust me out?"

"Well, I tried to, but I couldn't; I couldn't budge you."

"Well, all right. Don't stand there blabbing all day, but out with you and see if there's a fish on the lines for breakfast. I'll be along in a minute."

He unlocked the door and I cleared out, up the river bank. I noticed some pieces of branches and such things floating down, and a sprinkling of bark; so I knowed the river had begun to rise. I reckoned I would have great times, if I was over at the town. The June rise used to be always luck for me; because as soon as that rise begins, here comes wood floating down, and pieces of log rafts—sometimes a dozen logs together; so all you have to do is to catch them and sell them to the wood yards and the sawmill.

I went along up the riverbank with one eye out for Pap and 'tother one out for what the rise might fetch along. Well, all at once, here comes a canoe; just a beauty, too, about thirteen or fourteen foot long, riding high like a duck. I shot head first off of the bank, like a frog, clothes on, and struck out for the canoe. It was a drift-canoe, sure enough, and I clumb in and paddled her ashore. Thinks I, the old man will be glad when he sees this—she's worth ten dollars. But when I got to shore Pap wasn't in sight yet, and as I was running her into a little creek, like a gully, all hung over with vines and willows, I struck another idea; I judged I'd hide her good, and then, stead of taking to the woods when I run off, I'd go down the river about fifty mile and camp in one place for good, and not have such a rough time tramping on foot.

After breakfast, we laid off to sleep up, both of us

being about wore out. I got to thinking that if I could fix up some way to keep Pap and the widow from trying to follow me, it would be a certainer thing than trusting to luck to get far enough off before they missed me.

About twelve o'clock we got up and went along up the riverbank. The river was coming up pretty fast, and lots of driftwood going by. By-and-by, along comes part of a log raft—nine logs fast together. We went out with the rowboat and towed it ashore. Then we had dinner. Anybody but Pap would a waited and seen the day through, to catch more stuff; but that warn't Pap's style. Nine logs was enough for one time; he must shove right over to town and sell. So he locked me in and took the boat and started off towing the raft about half-past three. I waited till I reckoned he had got a good start, then I out with my saw and went to work on that log again. Before he was 'tother side of the river I was out of the hole; him and his raft was just a speck on the water away off yonder.

I took the sack of corn meal and took it to where the canoe was hid, and put it in; then I done the same with the side of bacon; then the whisky jug; I took all the coffee and sugar there was; I took the bucket, I took the dipper and a tin cup, and my old saw and two blankets, and the skillet and the coffee-pot. I took fish-lines and other things—everything that was worth a cent. I cleaned out the place. I wanted an axe, but there wasn't any, only the one out at the wood pile, and I knowed why I was going to leave that. I fetched out the gun, and now I was done. Then I fixed the piece of log back into place.

I stood on the bank and looked out over the river. All safe. So I took the gun and went up a piece into the woods and was hunting around for some birds, when I see a wild pig; hogs soon went wild in them bottoms

after they had got away from the prairie farms. I shot this fellow and took him into camp.

I took the axe and smashed in the door—I hacked it considerable a-doing it. I fetched the pig in and took him back nearly to the table and hacked into his throat with the axe, and laid him down on the ground to bleed. Well, last I pulled out some of my hair, and bloodied the axe good, and stuck it on the back side, and slung the axe in the corner. Then I took up the pig and held him to my breast with my jacket (so he couldn't drip) till I got a good piece below the house and then dumped him into the river.

It was about dark now, so I dropped the canoe down the river under some willows that hung over the bank, and waited for the moon to rise. I made fast to a willow; then I took a bite to eat, and by-and-by laid down in the canoe to smoke a pipe and lay out a plan. I says to myself, they'll drag the river for me. They'll soon get tired of that, and won't bother no more about me. I can stop anywhere I want to. Jackson's Island is good enough for me; I know that island pretty well, and nobody ever comes there. And then I can paddle over to town, nights, and slink around and pick up things I want.

It didn't take me long to get to Jackson's Island. I shot past the head at a ripping rate, the current was so swift, and then I got into the dead water and landed on the side towards the Illinois shore. I run the canoe into a deep dent in the bank that I knowed about; I had to part the willow branches to get in, and when I got in, nobody could a seen the canoe from the outside.

Chapter 3

In the morning I woke up pretty hungry, but it warn't going to do for me to start a fire, because the folks dragging the river for my carcass might see the smoke. The river was a mile wide there—so I was having a good enough time seeing them hunt for my remainders. That afternoon I got my traps out of the canoe and made me a nice camp in the thick woods. I made a kind of tent out of my blankets to put my things under so the rain couldn't get at them. I catched a catfish and haggled him open with my saw, and towards sundown I started my campfire and had supper. Then I set out a line to catch some fish for breakfast.

When it was dark I set by my campfire smoking, and feeling pretty satisfied; but by-and-by it got sort of lonesome, and so I went and set on the bank and listened to the currents washing along, and counted the stars and drift-logs and rafts that come down, and then went to bed; there ain't no better way to put in time when you are lonesome.

And so for three days and nights, no difference—just the same thing. But the next day I went exploring around down through the island. I was boss of it; it all belonged to me, so to say, and I wanted to know all about it. I found plenty strawberries, ripe and prime;

and green summer-grapes, and green raspberries; and the green blackberries was just beginning to show. Well, I went fooling along in the deep woods till I judged I warn't far from the foot of the island. All of a sudden I come right on to the ashes of a campfire that was still smoking.

My heart jumped up amongst my lungs. I never waited for to look further, but went sneaking back on my tiptoes as fast as ever I could. When I got to camp, I put all my traps into my canoe again so as to have them out of sight, and I put out the fire and scattered the ashes around to look like an old last year's camp, and then clumb a tree. I reckon I was up in the tree two hours; but I didn't see nothing, I didn't hear nothing—I only thought I heard and seen as much as a thousand things. Well, I couldn't stay up there forever, so at last I got down, saying to myself, I can't live this way; I'm agoing to find out who it is that's here on the island with me.

The next morning, just before daylight, I took my gun and slipped off to where I had run across that campfire. By-and-by I was close enough to have a look, and there laid a man on the ground. It most give me the fan-tods. He had a blanket around his head, and his head was nearly in the fire. I set there behind a clump of bushes, within about six foot of him, and kept my eyes on him steady. Pretty soon he stretched himself, and tossed off the blanket, and it was Miss Watson's Jim! I bet I was glad to see him. I says, "Hello, Jim!" and skipped out from my hiding place.

He bounced up and stared at me wild. Then he drops down on his knees and puts his hands together and says: "Doan hurt me—don't! I hain't ever done no harm to a ghos'. I alwuz liked dead people, en done all I could for 'em. You go git in de river agin, whah you b'longs, en doan' do nuffin to Ole Jim, that wuz alwuz yo' fren'."

Pretty soon he stretched himself,
and tossed off the blanket, and it was Miss Watson's Jim!

Well, I warn't long making him understand I warn't dead. Then I says, "Why, how long you been on the island, Jim?"

"I come heah de night arter you's killed.—How long you ben on de islan'?"

"Since the night I got killed."

"No! Now you go kill sumfin for breakfast, en I'll make up de fire."

So we went over to where the canoe was, and while he built the fire in a grassy open place amongst the trees, I fetched meal and bacon and coffee, and coffee-pot and frying-pan, and sugar and tin cups. I catched a good big catfish, too, and Jim cleaned him with his knife, and fried him.

Wnen breakfast was ready, we lolled on the grass and ate it smoking hot. Jim laid it in with all his might, for he was most about starved. Then when we had got pretty well stuffed, we laid off and lazied.

By-and-by Jim says: "But looky here, Huck, who wuz it dat 'uz killed in dat shanty, ef it warn't you?"

Then I told him the whole thing, and he said it was smart. He said Tom Sawyer couldn't get up no better plan than what I had. Then I says, "How do you come to be here, Jim, and how'd you get here?"

"Maybe I better not tell.—But you wouldn't tell on me ef I 'uz to tell you, would you?"

"Blamed if I would, Jim."

"Well, I b'lieve you, Huck. I—I *run off.*"

"Jim!"

"But mind, you said you wouldn't tell—you know you said you wouldn't tell, Huck."

"Well, I did. I said I wouldn't, and I'll stick to it. Honest injun I will. People would call me a low-down Abolitionist and despise me for keeping mum—but that don't make no difference. I ain't agoing to tell, and I ain't agoing back there anyways. So now, let's know all about it."

"Well, you see, it 'uz dis way. Ole Missus—dat's Miss Watson—she pecks on me all de time, en treats me pooty rough, but she alwuz said she wouldn't sell me down to New Orleans. But I noticed dey wuz a slave trader roun' de place considable lately, en I begin to git oneasy. Well, one night I creeps to de do', pooty late, en de do' warn't quite shet, en I hear Ole Missus tell de widder she gonna sell me down to Orleans. She didn't want to, but she could get eight hund'd dollars for me, en it 'uz sich a big stack o' money she couldn't resis'. De widder she try to git her to say she wouldn't do it, but I never waited to hear de res'. I lit out mighty quick,

I tell you. I tuck out en run down de hill to steal a boat 'long de sho' som'ers 'bove de town, but dey wuz people a-stirrin' yit, so I hid in de ole tumble-down cooper shop on de bank to wait for everybody to go 'way. Well, I wuz dah all night. 'Long 'bout six in de mawnin', skifts begin to go by, en 'bout eight er nine every boat dat went 'long wuz talkin' 'bout how yo' pap come over to de town en say you's killed. I 'uz powerful sorry you's killed, Huck, but I ain't no mo' now.

"When it comes dark again I tuck out up de river road, en went 'bout two mile or more to whah dey warn't no houses. I'd made up my mine 'bout what I's agonna do. You see ef I kep' on tryin' to git away afoot, de dogs 'ud track me; ef I stole a boat to cross over, dey'd miss dat skift, you see, en dey'd know 'bout whah I'd lan' on de yuther side en whah to pick up my track. So I says, a raff is what I's arter; it don't *make* no track. I see a light a-comin' 'roun de p'int, bymeby, so I wade' in en shove a log ahead o' me, en swum more'n halfway acrost the river, en got in 'mongst the driftwood, en kep' my head down low, en kinder swum agin the current tell a raff come along. Den I swum to de stern of it, en took aholt. When we 'uz mos' down to de head er de islan', a man come aft wid de lantern. I see it warn't no use, so I let go and struck out fer de islan'. I went into de wood en judged I wouldn't fool wid raffs no mo'. I had my pipe en a plug of tobacco, en some matches in my cap, en dey warn't wet, so I 'uz all right. Then I watched de ferryboat thoo de bushes."

We set and talked some more, then Jim, looking at the sky and listening to the birds, says it was fixing to rain that night. I wanted to go and look at a place right about the middle of the island, that I'd found when I was exploring; so we started, and soon got to it, because the island was only three miles long and a quarter of a mile wide.

The place was a tolerable long steep hill, about forty foot high. We had a rough time getting to the top, the sides was so steep and the bushes so thick. We tramped and clumb around all over it, and by-and-by found a good big cavern in the rock, most up to the top on the side toward Illinois. The cavern was as big as two or three rooms bunched together, and Jim could stand up straight in it. It was cool in there. Jim was for putting our traps inside, so we went back and got the canoe and paddled up abreast the cavern, and lugged all the traps up there. Then we hunted up a place close by to hide the canoe in, amongst the thick willows. We took some fish off of the lines and set them again, and begun to get ready for dinner.

On one side of the door of the cavern the floor stuck out a little bit and was flat and a good place to build a fire on. So we built it there and cooked dinner. We spread the blankets inside for a carpet, and eat our dinner in there. We put all the other things handy at the back of the cavern. Pretty soon it darkened up and begun to thunder and lightning. Soon it begun to rain, and it rained like fury, too, and I never see the wind blow so. It was one of these regular summer storms. It would get so dark that it looked all blue-black outside, and lovely; and the rain would thrash along by so thick that the trees off a little ways looked dim and spider-webby; and here would come a blast of wind that would bend the trees down and turn up the pale underside of the leaves.

"Jim, this is nice," I says. "I wouldn't want to be nowhere else but here. Pass me along another hunk of fish and some hot cornbread."

"Well, you wouldn't a ben here, if it hadn't a ben for Jim. You'd a ben down dah in de woods widout any dinner an gittin' mos' drownded, too, dat you would, honey."

"Jim, this is nice," I says.
"I wouldn't want to be nowhere else but here."

The river went on raising and raising for ten or twelve days, till at last it was over the banks. The water was three or four foot deep on the island in the low places. Daytimes we paddled all over the island in the canoe. It was mighty cool and shady in the deep woods even if the sun was blazing outside.

One night we catched a little section of a lumber raft—nice pine planks. It was twelve foot wide and about fifteen or sixteen foot long, and the top stood above water six or seven inches. Another night, when we was up at the head of the island, just before daylight, here comes a frame house down, on the west side. She was a two-story, and tilted over, considerable.

We paddled out and got aboard—clumb in at an upstairs window. But it was too dark to see yet, so we made the canoe fast and set in her to wait for daylight.

When the light begun to come up, we hurried to collect some goods. The way things was scattered about, we reckoned the people left in a hurry and warn't fixed so as to carry off most of their stuff. We got an old tin lantern, and a butcher knife without any handle, and a brand-new knife worth two bits in any store, and a lot of tallow candles, and a tin candlestick, and a gourd, and a tin cup, and a ratty old bedquilt off the bed, and a reticule with needles and pins and beeswax and buttons and thread and all such truck in it, and a hatchet and some nails, and a fishline as thick as my little finger, with some monstrous hooks on it, and a roll of buckskin, and a leather dog-collar, and a horseshoe, and some vials of medicine that didn't have no label on them; and just as we was leaving I found a tolerable good comb, and Jim he found a ratty old fiddlebow and a wooden leg. And so, take it all around, we made a good haul.

Then, just as we was leaving, Jim he found a body in one of the rooms. He told me not to look—it was a murdered man—says it was too scary and would cause nightmares. I didn't mind not looking.

Chapter 4

Well, the days went along, and the river went down between its banks again; I reckoned I would slip over the river and find out what was going on. Jim liked that notion; but he said I must go in the dark and look sharp. Then he studied it over and said, couldn't I put on some of them old things we'd found on the floated house and dress up like a girl? That was a good notion, so we shortened up one of the calico gowns and I turned up my trouser-legs to my knees and got into it. I put on a sunbonnet and tied it under my chin, and then for a body to look in and see my face was like looking down a stove-pipe. Jim said nobody would know me, not even in the daytime, hardly.

I started up the Illinois shore in the canoe just after dark across to the town from a little below the ferry landing, and the drift of the current fetched me in at the bottom of the town. I tied up and started along the bank. There was a light burning in a little shanty that hadn't been lived in for a long time, and I wondered who had took up quarters there. I slipped up and peeped in at the window. There was a woman about forty year old in there, knitting by a candle that was on a table. I didn't know her face; she was a stranger. Now this was lucky, because even if this woman had been in

I put on a sunbonnet and tied it under my chin.

such a little town two days she could tell me all I wanted to know; so I knocked at the door, and made up my mind I wouldn't forget I was a girl.

"Come in," says the woman, and I did. She says, "Take a cheer." I done it. She looked me all over and says, "What might your name be?"

"Sarah Williams."

"Where 'bouts do you live? In this neighborhood?"

"No'm. In Hookerville, seven mile below. I've walked all the way and I'm all tired out."

"Hungry, too, I reckon. I'll find you something."

"No'm, I ain't hungry. I was so hungry I had to stop two mile below here at a farm; so I ain't hungry no

more. It's what makes me so late. My mother's down sick, and out of money and everything, and I come to tell my uncle Abner Moore. He lives at the upper end of town, she says. I hain't never been here before. Do you know him?"

"No; but I don't know everybody yet. I haven't lived here quite two weeks. It's a considerable ways to the upper end of the town. You better stay here all night. Take off your bonnet."

"No," I says, "I'll rest a while, I reckon, and go on. I ain't afeared of the dark.

She said she wouldn't let me go by myself, but her husband would be in by-and-by, maybe in an hour and a half, and she'd send him along with me. Then she got to talking about Pap and the murder, and that some was thinking Pap killed Huck Finn, and some judged it was Miss Watson's slave Jim! Both of them had disappeared the night I was killed, and there was reward money for both.

"A good many thinks the slave done it," she says. "But they'll get him pretty soon, now, and maybe they can scare the truth out of him."

"Why, are they after him still?"

"Does three hundred dollars lay round every day for people to pick up? Some folks think that slave ain't far from here. I'm one of them—but I hain't talked it around. A few days ago I was talking with an old couple that lives next door to that island over yonder that they call Jackson's Island. Don't anybody live there, says I. No, nobody, says they. I didn't say any more, but I done some thinking. I was pretty near certain I'd seen smoke over there, about the head of the island, a day or two before that, so I says to myself, like as not that slave's hiding over there; anyway, says I, it's worth the trouble to give the place a hunt. My husband's going over to

see—him and another man. They'll go over after midnight."

I had got so uneasy I couldn't set still. I told her I had to go now, and she tried to keep me, but I says it was important for my mother. I hurried away and slipped back to where my canoe was, a good piece below the house. I jumped in and was off in a hurry. When I landed, I slopped through the timber and up the ridge and into the cavern. There Jim laid, sound asleep on the ground. I roused him out and says: "Git up and hurry yourself, Jim! There ain't a minute to lose. They're after us!"

He never asked no questions, he never said a word; but the way he worked for the next half an hour showed about how he was scared. By that time everything we had in the world was on our raft and she was ready to be shoved out from the willow cover where she was hid. We put out the campfire at the cavern the first thing, and didn't show a candle after that.

I took the canoe out from the shore a little piece and took a look, but if there was a boat around I couldn't see it, for stars and shadows ain't good to see by. Then we got out the raft and slipped along down in the shade, past the foot of the island dead still, never saying a word.

When the first streak of day begun to show, we tied up to a wooded sandbar in a big bend on the Illinois side, and hacked off cottonwood branches with the hatchet and covered up the raft with them. We laid there all day and watched the rafts and steamboats spin down the Missouri shore, and upbound steamboats fight the big river in the middle. When it was beginning to come on dark, we poked our heads out of the cottonwood thicket and looked up and down and across. Nothing in sight. So Jim took up some of the top

We laid there all day and watched the rafts and steamboats spin down the Missouri shore, and upbound steamboats fight the big river in the middle.

planks of the raft and built a snug wigwam to get under in blazing weather and rainy, and to keep things dry. Jim made a floor for the wigwam, and raised it a foot or more above the level of the raft, so now the blankets and all the traps was out of the reach of steamboat waves. Right in the middle of the wigwam we made a layer of dirt about five or six inches deep with a frame around it for to hold it to its place; this was to build a fire on in sloppy weather or chilly; the wigwam would keep it from being seen.

This second night we run between seven and eight hours, with a current that was making over four mile an hour. We catched fish, and talked, and we took a swim

now and then to keep off sleepiness. We had mighty good weather, as a general thing, and nothing ever happened to us at all, that night, nor the next, nor the next several.

Every night we passed towns, some of them away up on black hillsides, nothing but just a shiny bed of lights, not a house could you see. The fifth night we passed St. Louis, and it was like the whole world lit up. But there warn't a sound there; everybody was asleep. Every night now I used to slip ashore, towards ten o'clock, at some little village, and buy ten or fifteen cents' worth of meal or bacon or other stuff to eat; and sometimes I lifted a chicken and took him along.

Mornings, before daylight, I slipped into corn fields and borrowed a watermelon, or a mushmelon, or a punkin, or some new corn, or things of that kind. Pap always said it warn't no harm to borrow things, if you was meaning to pay them back, sometime; but the widow said it warn't anything but a soft name for stealing, and no decent body would do it. We shot a waterfowl, now and then. Take it all around, we lived pretty high.

The fifth night below St. Louis we had a big storm after midnight, with a power of thunder and lightning, and the rain poured down in a solid sheet. We stayed in the wigwam and let the raft take care of itself. When the lightning glared out we could see a big straight river ahead, and high rocky bluffs on both sides. By-and-by the sky was beginning to get a little gray in the east; so we struck for an island and hid the raft, and turned in and slept like dead people.

When we got up, we judged that three nights more would fetch us to Cairo, at the bottom of the Illinois, where the Ohio River comes in, and that was what we was after. We would sell the raft and get on a steamboat

and go way up the Ohio amongst the free States, and then be out of trouble.

Well, the second night a fog begun to come on, and we made for a towhead to tie to, for it wouldn't do to try to run in fog; but when I paddled ahead in the canoe, with the line, to make fast, there warn't anything but little saplings to tie to. So I tied up the best I could, and hoped for the best. Then I come back to the raft. When I waked up the stars was shining bright, the fog was all gone, and we was spinning down a big bend stern first. First I didn't know where I was; I thought I was dreaming; and when things begun to come back to me, they seemed to come up dim out of last week. We musta broke free of the tie-up.

It was a monstrous big river here, with the tallest and the thickest kind of timber on both banks. Then we found a place to tie up the raft again. We slept most all day, and started out at night, drifting down into a big bend, where the night clouded up and got hot. The river was very wide, and was walled with solid timber on both sides; you couldn't see a break in it hardly ever, or a light. We talked about Cairo, Illinois, and wondered whether we would know it when we got to it. I said likely we wouldn't, because I had heard say there warn't but about a dozen houses there, and if they didn't happen to have them lit up, how was we going to know we was passing a town? Jim said if the two big rivers joined together there, that would show. But I said maybe we might think we was passing the foot of an island, and coming into the same old river again. That disturbed Jim—and me, too.

There warn't nothing to do but to look out sharp for the town, and not pass it without seeing it. He said he'd be mighty sure to see it, because he'd be a free man the minute he seen it, but if he missed it he'd be in the slave

country again and no more show for freedom. Every little while he jumps up and says:

"Dah she is!"

But it warn't. It was Jack-o-lanterns, or lightning bugs; so he set down again, and went to watching, same as before. We neither of us could keep still. Every time he danced around and says, "Dah's Cairo!" it went through me like a shot. Jim talked out loud all the time while I was talking to myself. I'm helping a slave run away! Meantime, Jim he was saying how the first thing he would do when he got to a free state he would go to saving up money and never spend a single cent, and when he got enough he would buy his wife, which was owned on a farm close to where Miss Watson lived; and then they would both work to buy the two children, and if their master wouldn't sell them, they'd get an Abolitionist to go and steal them.

Jim sings out: "We's safe, Huck, we's safe! Jump up and crack yo' heels, dat's de good ole Cairo at las', I jis knows it!"

I says: "I'll take the canoe and go see, Jim. It mightn't be, you know."

He jumped and got the canoe ready, and put his old coat in the bottom for me to set on, and give me the paddle; and as I shoved off, he says, "Pooty soon I'll be a-shoutin' for joy, en I'll say, it's all on accounts o' Huck; I's a free man, en I couldn't ever ben free ef it hadn't ben for Huck; Huck done it. Jim won't ever forgit you, Huck; you's de bes' fren' Jim ever had; en you's de *only* fren' ole Jim's got now."

When I was fifty yards off, Jim says, "Dah you goes, de ole true Huck; de on'y white genlman dat ever kep' his promise to ole Jim."

Well, the light warn't nothing but a wood-yard, and there was no houses about, so I paddled back to the

raft. Jim was sore disappointed. Towards daybreak we tied up, and Jim was mighty particular about hiding the raft good. But then, when it was full light, we saw below us the clear Ohio water in shore, and outside was the old regular muddy! So we had already passed Cairo!

"Maybe we went by Cairo in the fog that night."

He says: "Doan less' talk about it, Huck. Po' Jim can't have no luck. Don't you blame yo'self 'bout it."

We talked it all over. It wouldn't do to take to the shore; we couldn't take the raft up the stream, of course. There warn't no way but to wait for dark, and start back in the canoe and take our chances. So we slept all day amongst the cottonwood thicket, so as to be fresh for the work, and when we went back to the raft about dark the canoe was gone!

By-and-by we talked about what we better do, and found there warn't no way but just to go along down with the raft till we got a chance to buy a canoe to go back in.

Chapter 5

Two or three days and nights went by; I reckon I might say they swum by, they slid along so quiet and smooth and lovely. We said there warn't no home like a raft. Other places do seem so cramped up and smothery, but a raft don't. You feel mighty free and easy and comfortable on a raft.

Here is the way we put in the time. It was a monstrous big river down there—sometimes a mile and a half wide; we run nights, and laid up and hid daytimes; soon as night was most gone, we stopped navigating and tied up—nearly always in the dead water under a towhead; and then cut young cottonwoods and willows and hid the raft with them. Then we set out the lines. Next we slid into the river and had a swim, so as to freshen up and cool off; then we set down on the sandy bottom where the water was about knee deep, and watched the daylight come. Not a sound, anywheres—perfectly still—just like the whole world was asleep, only sometimes the bullfrogs a-cluttering maybe. The first thing to see, looking away over the water, was a kind of dull line—that was the woods on t'other side—you couldn't make nothing else out; then a pale place in the sky; then more paleness, spreading around; then the river softened up, away off, and warn't black any

more, but gray; you could see little dark spots drifting along, ever so far away; and next you've got the full day, and everything smiling in the sun, and the songbirds just going it!

A little smoke couldn't be noticed, now, so we would take some fish off of the lines, and cook up a hot breakfast. And afterwards we would watch the lonesomeness of the river, and kind of lazy along; and by-and-by lazy off to sleep. Wake up, by-and-by, and maybe see a steamboat, coughing along upstream. Next you'd see a raft sliding by, away off yonder. So we put in the day, lazying around, listening to the stillness.

Soon as it was night, out we shoved; when we got her out to about the middle, we let her alone, and let her float wherever the current wanted to; then we lit the pipes, and dangled our legs in the water and talked about all kinds of things—we was always naked, day and night, whenever the mosquitoes would let us.

Sometimes we'd have that whole river all to ourselves for the longest time. Yonder was the banks and the islands, across the water; and maybe a spark—which was a candle in a cabin window—and sometimes on the water you could see a spark or two—on a raft or scow, you know; and maybe you could hear a fiddle or a song coming over from one of them rafts. It's lovely to live on a raft. We had the sky, up there, all speckled with stars, and we used to lay on our backs and look up at them, and discuss about whether they was made, or only just happened. We used to watch the stars that fell, too, and see them streak down.

Once or twice of a night we would see a steamboat slipping along in the dark, and now and then she would belch a whole world of sparks up out of her chimneys, and they would rain down in the river and look awful pretty; and by-and-by her waves would get to us, a long

time after she was gone, and joggle the raft a bit, and after that you wouldn't hear nothing for you couldn't tell how long, except maybe frogs or something.

After midnight the people on shore went to bed, and then for two or three hours the shores was black—no more sparks in the cabin windows. These sparks was our clock—the first one that showed again meant morning was coming, so we hunted a place to hide and tie up, right away.

One morning about daybreak, I found a canoe and crossed over to the main shore, and paddled up a crick amongst the cypress woods, to see if I couldn't get some berries. Just as I was passing a place where a kind of cowpath crossed the crick, here comes a couple of men tearing up the path as tight as they could foot it. They sung out and begged me to save their lives—said they hadn't been doing nothing and was being chased for it—said there was men and dogs a-coming. Soon as they was aboard I lit out for our towhead.

One of these fellows was about seventy, or upwards, and had a bald head and very gray whiskers. He had an old long-tailed blue jeans coat with slick brass buttons, flung over his arm, and both of them had big fat ratty-looking carpetbags.

The other fellow was about thirty and dressed about as ornery. After breakfast we all laid off and talked, and the first thing that come out was that these chaps didn't know one another.

"What got you into trouble?" says the baldhead to the other chap.

"Well, I'd been selling an article to take the tartar off the teeth—and it does take it off, too, and generly the enamel along with it—but I stayed about one night longer than I ought to. What's your trouble?"

"Well, I'd been a-runnin' a little temperance revival

They sung out and begged me to save their lives.

thar, 'bout a week, and was the pet of the women-folks, big and little, for I was makin' it mighty warm for the rummies, I tell you, and takin' as much as five or six dollars a night—and business a-growin' all the time; when somehow or another a little report got around, last night, that I had a way of puttin' in my time with a private jug, on the sly. They said they'd tar and feather me if they caught me, so I didn't wait for no breakfast—I warn't hungry."

"Old man," says the young one, "I reckon we might double-team it together; what do you think?"

"I ain't undisposed."

By-and-by the young one says, "I brought myself down—yes, I did it myself."

"Brought you down from whar?" says the baldhead. "Whar was you brought down from?"

"Ah, you would not believe me; the world never believes—let it pass—'tis no matter. The secret of my birth!"

"Ah, come on and tell us," says the bald man.

"Very well," says the younger man. "Gentlemen, I will reveal this startling secret to you. By rights I am a duke!"

Jim's eyes bugged out when he heard that; and I reckon mine did too. Then the baldhead man says, "No! You can't mean it?"

"Yes, my great-grandfather, eldest son of the Duke of Bridgewater, fled to this country about the end of the last century, to breathe the pure air of freedom; married here, and died, leaving a son, his own father dying about that same time. The second son of the late duke seized the title and estates—the infant real duke was ignored. I am the descendant of that infant—I am the rightful Duke of Bridgewater, and here I am, degraded to the companionship of felons on a raft!"

Jim pitied him ever so much, and so did I.

He said we ought to bow, when we spoke to him, and say, "Your Grace," or "My Lord," or "Your Lordship"; and one of us ought to wait on him at dinner, and do any little thing for him he wanted done.

The old man got pretty silent, by-and-by. He seemed to have something on his mind. So, along in the afternoon, he says, "Look here, Bilgewater, I'm nation sorry for you, but you ain't the only person that's had troubles like that."

"No?"

"No, you ain't the only person that's had a secret of his birth." And by jings, *he* begins to cry. "Your eyes is lookin' at this very moment on the pore disappeared

oldest son of the King of France, Lewis the Seventeen, son of Lewis the Sixteen and Marry Antonette. Yes, gentlemen, you see before you, in blue jeans and misery, the wanderin', exiled, trampled-on and sufferin' rightful King of France."

Well, he cried and took on so, that me and Jim didn't know hardly what to do, we was so sorry—and so glad and proud we'd got him with us, too. So we set in, like we done before with the duke, and tried to comfort *him*. But the duke didn't look a bit satisfied with the way things was going.

By-and-by the king says, "Like as not we got to be together a blamed long time, on this h'yer raft, Bilgewater, and so what's the use o' your bein' sour? It'll only make things oncomfortable."

"Make the best o' things the way you find 'em," says I. "This ain't no bad thing that we've struck here—plenty grub and an easy life—come, give us your hand, duke, and less all be friends."

The duke done it, and Jim and me was pretty glad to see it. It would a been a miserable business to have any unfriendliness on the raft; for what you want, above all things, on a raft, is for everybody to be satisfied, and feel right and kind towards the others.

It didn't take me long, though, to make up my mind that these liars warn't no kings nor dukes, at all, but just low-down humbugs and frauds. But I never said nothing, never let on; it's the best way; then you don't have no quarrels, and don't get into no trouble. If they wanted us to call them kings and dukes, I hadn't no objections, 'long as it would keep peace in the family; and it warn't no use to tell Jim, so I didn't tell him.

They asked us considerable many questions; wanted to know what we covered up the raft that way for, and laid by in the daytime instead of running—was Jim a

runaway slave? Says I, "Goodness sakes, would a runaway slave run *south*?"

No, they allowed he wouldn't.

Towards night it begun to darken up and look like rain; the heat lightning was squirting around, low down in the sky, and the leaves was beginning to shiver—it was going to be pretty ugly, it was easy to see that. About ten o'clock it come on to rain and blow and thunder and lighten like everything; so the king told us to both stay on watch till the weather got better; then him and the duke crawled into the wigwam and turned in for the night. It was my watch below, till twelve, but I wouldn't a turned in, anyway, if I'd had a bed; because a body don't see such a storm as that every day in the week, not by a long sight. My souls, how the wind did scream along! And every second or two there'd come a glare that lit up the whitecaps for a half a mile around, and you'd see the islands looking dusty through the rain, and the trees thrashing around in the wind; then comes a *h-wack!*—bum! bum! bumble-umble-um-bum-bum-bum-bum—and the thunder would go rumbling and grumbling away, and quit—and then *rip* comes another flash and another sockdolager. The waves most washed me off the raft, sometimes, but I hadn't any clothes on, and didn't mind. We didn't have no trouble with snags; the lightning was glaring and flittering around so constant that we could see them plenty soon enough to throw her head this way or that and miss them.

I had the middle watch, you know, but I was pretty sleepy by that time, so Jim he said he would stand the first half of it for me; he was always mighty good that way, Jim was. I crawled into the wigwam, but the king and the duke had their legs sprawled around so there warn't no show for me; so I laid outside—I didn't mind

the rain, because it was warm, and the waves warn't running so high, now.

Jim didn't call me when it was my turn. He often done that. When I waked up, just at daybreak, he was setting there with his head down betwixt his knees, moaning and mourning to himself. I didn't take no notice, nor let on. I knowed what it was about. He was thinking about his wife and his children, away up yonder, and he was so low and homesick; because he hadn't ever been away from home before in his life; and I do believe he cared just as much for his people as white folks does for their'n. It don't seem natural, but I reckon it's so. He was often moaning and mourning that way, nights, when he judged I was asleep, and saying, "Po' little 'Lizabeth! po' little Johnny! I spec' I ain't ever gonna see you no mo', no mo'!"

Chapter 6

We didn't stop at any town, for days and days; kept right along down the river. We was down south in the warm weather, now, and a mighty long ways from home. We begun to come to trees with Spanish moss on them, hanging down from the limbs like long gray beards. It was the first I ever see it growing, and it made the woods look solemn and dismal. So now the frauds reckoned they were out of danger, and they begun to work the villages.

First they done a lecture on temperance—the evils of drinking liquor—but they didn't make enough for them both to get drunk on. Then in another village they started a dancing school; but they didn't know no more how to dance than a kangaroo does; so the first prance they made, the general public jumped in and pranced them out of town. They tackled missionarying, and mesmerizering, and doctoring, and telling fortunes, and a little of everything; but they couldn't seem to have no luck. So at last they got just about dead broke, and laid around the raft, as she floated along, thinking, and thinking, and never saying nothing, by the half a day at a time, and dreadful blue and desperate.

And at last they took a change, and began to lay their heads together in the wigwam and talk low and confi-

dential two or three hours at a time. Jim and me got uneasy. We didn't like the look of it. We judged they was studying up some kind of worst deviltry than ever. We turned it over and over, and at last we made up our

We begun to come to trees with Spanish moss on them, hanging down from the limbs like long gray beards.

minds they was going to break into somebody's house or store, or was going into the counterfeit money business, or something. So then we was pretty scared, and made up an agreement that we wouldn't have nothing

to do with such actions, and if we ever got the least show we would give them the cold shake, and clear out and leave them behind. Well, early one morning we hid the raft in a good safe place about two mile below a bit of a shabby village named Pikesville, and the king went ashore, and told us all to stay hid whilst we went up to town and smelt around to see if anybody had got any wind of them there yet. ("House to rob, you mean," says I to myself; "and when you get through robbing it you'll come back here and wonder what's become of me and Jim and the raft—and you'll have to take it out in wondering.") And he said if we warn't back by midday, the duke and me would know it was all right, and we was to come along.

So we stayed where we was. The duke he fretted and sweated around, and was in a mighty sour way. He scolded us for everything, and we couldn't seem to do nothing right; he found fault with every little thing. Something was a-brewing, sure. I was good and glad when midday come and no king; we could have a change, anyway—and maybe a chance for *the* change, on top of it. So me and the duke went up to the village, and hunted around there for the king, and by-and-by we found him in the back room of a tavern, very drunk, and a lot of loafers bullyragging him for sport, and he a-cussing and threatening with all his might, and so drunk he couldn't walk, and couldn't do nothing to them. The duke he begun to call him an old fool, and the king begun to sass back; and the minute they was fairly at it, I lit out, and spun down the river road like a deer—for I see our chance; and I made up my mind that it would be a long day before they ever see me and Jim again. I got down there all out of breath but loaded up with joy, and sung out, "Set her loose, Jim, we're all right, now!"

But there warn't no answer, and nobody come out of the wigwam. Jim was gone! I set up a shout—and then another—and then another one; and run this way and that in the woods, whooping and screeching; but it warn't no use—old Jim was gone. Pretty soon I went out on the road, trying to think what I better do, and I run across a boy walking, and asked him if he'd seen a strange slave, dressed so and so, and he says, "Yes."

"Whereabouts?" says I.

"Down to Silas Phelps's place, two mile below here. He's a runaway slave, and they've got him. Was you looking for him?"

"You bet I ain't! I run across him in the woods about an hour or two ago, and he said if I hollered he'd cut my livers out."

"Well," he says, "you needn't be afeard no more, becuz they've got him. There's three hundred dollars reward on him. It's like picking up money out'n the road."

"Yes, it is—and *I* could a had it if I'd been big enough; I see him first. Who nailed him?"

"It was an old fellow—a stranger—and he sold out his chance in him for forty dollars, becuz he's got to go up the river and can't wait."

I went to the raft, and set down in the wigwam to think. But I couldn't come to nothing. I thought till I wore my head sore, but I couldn't see no way out of the trouble. After all this long journey, and after all we'd done for them scoundrels, here was it all come to nothing, everything all busted up and ruined, because they could have the heart to serve Jim such a trick as that, and make him a slave agin all his life, and amongst strangers, for forty dirty dollars.

I would go and steal Jim out of slavery again. Then I set to thinking over how to get at it, and turned over

considerable many ways in my mind; and at last fixed up a plan that suited me. So then I took the bearings of a woody island that was down the river a piece, and as soon as it was fairly dark I crept out with my raft and went for it, and hid it there, and then turned in. I slept the night through, and got up before it was light, and had my breakfast, and put on my best clothes, and tied up some others and one thing or another in a bundle, and took the canoe and cleared for shore. I landed below where I judged was Phelps's place, and hid my bundle in the woods, and then filled up the canoe with water, and loaded rocks into her and sunk her where I could find her again when I wanted her, about a quarter of a mile below a little stream that was on the bank.

Chapter 7

Then I struck up the road, and when I passed the mill I see a sign on it, "Phelps's Sawmill," and when I come to the farmhouses, I kept my eyes peeled, but didn't see nobody around.

Phelps's was one of these little one-horse cotton plantations; and they all look alike. A rail fence round a two-acre yard; some sickly grass-patches in the big yard, but mostly it was bare and smooth, like an old hat with nap rubbed off; big double loghouse for the white folks—hewed logs, with the chinks stopped up with mud; round-log kitchen, with a big broad, open but roofed passage joining it to the house; log smokehouse back of the kitchen; three little log slave-cabins in a row the other side the smokehouse; one little hut all by itself away down against the back fence, and some outbuildings down a piece the other side; bench by the kitchen door; hound asleep there, in the sun; more hounds asleep, round about; about three shade-trees away off in a corner; some currant bushes and gooseberry bushes in one place by the fence; outside of the fence a garden and a watermelon patch; then the cotton fields begin; and after the fields, the woods.

I went around and clumb over the back stile by the ash-hopper, and started for the kitchen. When I got a lit-

Phelps's was one of these little one-horse cotton plantations; and they all look alike.

tle ways, I heard the dim hum of a spinning-wheel wailing along and sinking along down again. I went right along, not fixing up any particular plan, but just trusting to Providence to put the right words in my mouth when the time come; for I'd noticed that Providence always did put the right words in my mouth, if I left it alone.

When I got halfway, first one hound and then another got up and went for me, and of course I stopped and faced them, and kept still. And such another pow-wow as they made! In a quarter of a minute I was a kind of hub of a wheel, as you may say—spokes made out of dogs—circle of fifteen of them packed together around me, with their necks and noses stretched up towards me, a-barking and howling; and more a-coming; you could see them sailing over fences and around corners from everywheres.

Here comes a white woman running from the house, about forty-five or fifty year old, bareheaded, and her spinning-stick in her hand; and behind her comes her little children. She was smiling all over so could hardly stand—and says, "It's *you,* at last!—*ain't* it?"

I out with a "Yes'm," before I thought.

She grabbed me and hugged me tight; and then gripped me by both hands and shook and shook; and the tears come in her eyes, and run down over, and she saying, "You don't look as much like your mother as I reckoned you would, but law sakes, I don't care for that, I'm so glad to see you! Children, it's your cousin Tom!—tell him howdy."

But they ducked their heads and put their fingers in their mouths, and hid behind her. So she run on: "You hain't told me a word about Sis, nor any of them. Now just tell your Aunt Sally *everything*—tell me all about 'em all—every one of 'em; and how they are, and what they're doing, and what they told you to tell me; and every last thing you can think of."

Well, I see I was up a stump—and up it good. Providence had stood by me this fur, all right, but I was hard and tight aground now. I see it warn't a bit of use to try to go ahead—I'd *got* to throw up my hand. So I says to myself, here's another place where I got to resk

the truth. I opened my mouth to begin; but she grabbed me and hustled me in behind the bed, and says: "Here comes your uncle Silas! Stick your head down lower—there, that'll do; you can't be seen now. I'll play a joke on him. Children, don't say a word."

I see I was in a fix, now. But it warn't no use to worry; there warn't nothing to do but just hold still. Mrs. Phelps she jumps for him and says, "Has he come on the boat?"

"No," says her husband.

"He must a come; and you've missed him along the road. I *know* it's so—something *tells* me so."

"But there's no hope that he's come; for he *couldn't* come and me miss him. Sally, it's terrible—just terrible—something's happened to the boat, sure!"

"Why, Silas! Look yonder!—up the road!—ain't that somebody coming?"

He sprung to the window, and that gave Mrs. Phelps the chance she wanted. She stooped down quick, and give me a pull, and out I come. And when he turned back from the window, there she stood, a-beaming and a-smiling like a house afire, and I standing pretty meek and sweaty alongside. The old gentleman stared and says, "Why, who's that?"

"Who do you reckon 'tis? It's *Tom Sawyer!*"

By jings, I most slumped through the floor. The old man grabbed me by the hand and shook, and kept on shaking; and all the time, how the woman did dance around and laugh and cry; and then how they both did fire off questions about Sid, and Mary, and the rest of the tribe.

But if they was joyful, it warn't nothing to what I was; for it was like being born again, I was so glad to find out who I was. Well, they froze to me for two hours; and at last when my chin was so tired it couldn't hardly go any

more, I had told them more about my family—I mean the Sawyer family—than ever happened to any six Sawyer families.

Now I was feeling pretty comfortable all down one side, and pretty uncomfortable all up the other. Being Tom Sawyer was easy and comfortable; and it stayed easy and comfortable till by-and-by I hear a steamboat coughing along down the river—then I says to myself, spose Tom Sawyer come down on that boat?—and spose he steps in here, any minute, and sings out my name before I can throw him a wink to keep quiet? Well, I couldn't have it that way. I must go up the road and waylay him. So I told the folks I reckoned I would go up to the town and fetch down my baggage.

So I started for town, and when I was halfway I see a wagon coming; and sure enough it was Tom Sawyer, and I stopped and waited till he come along. I says, "Hold on!" and it stopped alongside, and his mouth opened up like a trunk, and stayed so; and he swallowed two or three times like a person that's got a dry throat, and then says: "I hain't ever done you no harm. You know that. So then, what you want to come back and haunt *me* for?"

I says, "I hain't come back—I hain't been *gone.*"

When he heard my voice, it righted him up some, but he warn't quite satisfied yet. He says, "Don't you play nothing on me, because I wouldn't on you. Honest injun, now, you ain't a ghost?"

"Honest injun, I ain't," I says.

"Well—I—I—well, that ought to settle it, of course; but I can't somehow seem to understand it, no way. Looky here, warn't you ever murdered *at all*?"

"No. I warn't ever murdered at all—I played it on them. You come in here and feel of me if you don't believe me."

So he done it; and it satisfied him; and he was that glad to see me again, he didn't know what to do. And he wanted to know all about it right off; because it was a grand adventure, and mysterious, and so it hit him where he lived. I told him the kind of fix I was in, and what did he reckon we better do? So he thought and thought, and pretty soon he says, "It's all right, I've got it. I'll play I'm my brother Sid."

"All right; but wait a minute. There's one more thing—a thing that *nobody* don't know but me. And that is, there's someone here that I'm a-trying to steal out of slavery—and his name is *Jim*—old Miss Watson's Jim."

He says, "What! Why Jim is—"

He stopped and went to studying. I says: "I know what you'll say. You'll say slave-stealing's a dirty low-down business; but what if it is—*I'm* low-down; and I'm a-going to steal him, and I want you to keep mum and not let on. Will you?"

His eye lit up and he says, "I'll *help* you steal him!"

"Oh, shucks," I says, "you're joking."

"I ain't joking, either."

In about half an hour our wagon drove up to the front stile, and Aunt Sally she see us through the window, and says, "Why, there's somebody come with Tom! I wonder who 'tis? Jimmy" (that's one of the children), "Run and tell Lize to put on another plate for dinner."

Everybody made a rush for the front door. Tom jumped out and went up to Aunt Sally and kissed her right on the mouth.

"You owdacious puppy!"

He looked kind of hurt, and says, "I'm surprised at you, m'am."

"What do you mean by kissing me!"

"I didn't mean nothing, m'am. I—I—thought you'd like it. They told me you would."

"Who's *they*?"

Tom looks on around to me and says, "Tom, didn't you think Aunt Sally'd open out her arms and say, 'Sid Sawyer—'"

"My land!" she says, breaking in and jumping for him, "you young rascal, to fool a body so!" and she hugged him, and kissed him, over and over again. And after they got a little quiet again, she says, "Why, dear me, I never see such a surprise. We warn't looking for you, but only Tom. Sis never wrote to me about anybody coming but him."

"It's because it warn't *intended* for any of us to come but Tom," he says; "but I begged and begged, and at the last minute she let me come, too; so, coming down the river, me and Tom thought it would be a first-rate surprise for him to come here to the house first, and for me to by-and-by fetch a wagon and drop in and let on to be a stranger."

We had dinner out in that broad open passage betwixt the house and the kitchen; and there was things enough on that table for seven families. Uncle Silas, he's a farmer and a preacher, well, he asked a pretty long blessing over it, but it was worth it.

At supper, at night, one of the little boys says, "Pa, mayn't Tom and Sid and me go to the show?"

"No," says the old man, "I reckon there ain't going to be any; and you couldn't go there if there was; because the runaway slave told Burton and me all about those two scandalous frauds he was with, and Burton said he would tell the people; so I reckon they've drove the owdacious loafers out of town before this time."

So there it was!—but I couldn't help it. I was sorry for the duke and the king, those poor pitiful rascals.

That night, in our room, Tom and me was talking, telling each other about the adventures we'd had, when

by-and-by Tom says, "Looky, here, Huck, what fools we are, to not think of it before! I bet I know where Jim is!"

"No! Where?"

"In that hut down by the ash-hopper. Why, when we was at dinner, didn't you see a slave-man go in there with some vittles? It shows how a body can see and don't see at the same time. He unlocked the padlock when he went in, and he locked it again when he come out. He fetched Uncle Silas the key. All right—I'm glad we found it out. Now you work your mind and study out a plan to steal Jim, and I will study out one, too; and we'll take the one we like the best."

I went to thinking out a plan, but only just to be doing something; I knowed very well where the right plan was coming from. Pretty soon, Tom says, "Ready?"

"My plan is this," I says. "We can easy find out if it's Jim in there. Then get up my canoe tomorrow night, and fetch my raft over from the island. Then the first dark night that comes, steal the key out of the old man's britches, after he goes to bed, and shove off down the river on the raft, with Jim, hiding daytimes and running nights, the way me and Jim used to do before. Wouldn't that plan work?"

"*Work?* Why certainly it would *work*. But it's too blame simple; there ain't nothing to it. What's the good of a plan that ain't no more trouble than that? Why, Huck, it wouldn't make no more talk than breaking into a soap factory."

He told me what his plan was, and I see in a minute it was worth fifteen of mine, for style, and would make Jim just as free a man as mine would, and maybe get us all killed besides. So I was satisfied, and said we would waltz in on it. I needn't tell what it was, here, because I knowed it wouldn't stay the way it was. I knowed he would be changing it around, every which way, as we

went along, and heaving in new clevernesses whenever he got the chance. And that is what he done.

By the time we was done investigating the cabin (it was Jim in there, sure enough), Tom says, "Blame it, this whole thing is just as easy as it can be. And it makes it so rotten difficult to get up a difficult plan. There ain't no watchman to be drugged—now there *ought* to be a watchman. There ain't even a dog to give the sleeping mixture to. And there's Jim chained by one leg, with a ten-foot chain, to the leg of his bed: why, all you got to do is to lift up the bedstead and slip off the chain. And Uncle Silas trusts everybody; sends the key to his slave, and don't send nobody to watch the slave. Jim could a got out of that cabin's window-hole before this, only there wouldn't be no use trying to travel with a ten-foot chain on his leg. Why, drat it, Huck, it's the stupidest arrangement I ever see. You got to invent all the difficulties."

That night, Tom and me went down the lightning-rod from our room a little after ten, and took one of the candles along, and listened under the window-hole, and heard Jim snoring; so we whirled in with a pick and shovel, and in about two hours and a half the job was done. We crept in under Jim's bed and into the cabin, and pawed around and found the candle we'd already snuck to him, and stood over Jim a while, and then we woke him up gentle and gradual. He was so glad to see us he most cried; and called us honey, and all the pet names he could think of; and was for having us hunt up a cold chisel to cut the chain off his leg with, right away, and clearing out without losing any time. But Tom showed him how unregular it would be, and set down and told him all about our plans, and how we could alter them in a minute any time there was an alarm; and not to be the least afraid, because we would see he got away, *sure*. So Jim he said it was all right, and

we set there and talked over old times a while. Jim had plenty corn-cob pipes and tobacco; so we had a right down good sociable time; then we crawled out through the hole, and so home to bed, with hands that looked like they'd been chawed.

Well, to make a long story short, we did nearly get killed trying to set Jim free. What with all our difficulty-making, by a week or so later, we had made so much suspicion arise a gang of cutthroats was going to steal Jim that Uncle Silas had men with rifles and hunting dogs all abouts the farm. Nobody knew it was us when we was running off with Jim through the woods, so they fired plenty of times. It would've been dandy, except for Tom getting hurt, a bullet right in the calf.

We laid him in the wigwam on the raft and tore up one of the duke's shirts for to bandage him. Tom was all for us heading off down the river, but me and Jim was consulting—and thinking. And after we'd thought a minute, I says: "Say it, Jim."

So he says: "Well, den, dis is de way it look to me, Huck. Ef it wuz *him* dat 'uz bein' sot free, en one er de boys wuz to git shot, would he say, 'Go on en save me, nemmine 'bout a doctor for to save dis one?' You *bet* he wouldn't! Well, den, is *Jim* gonna say it? No, sah—I doan' budge a step out'n dis place, 'dout a *doctor*; not if it's forty year!"

I told Tom I was agoing for a doctor. He raised considerable row about it, but me and Jim stuck to it; so he was for crawling out and setting the raft loose himself; but we wouldn't let him. So I set out in the canoe for the village, and Jim was to hide in the woods when he see the doctor coming, till he was gone again. By the time I got back with the doctor, Tom was nearly out of his head with pain and suffering, and Jim stayed there doing all he could to nurse him, and didn't leave or hide. The doctor he figured out that Jim was the run-

away slave. When we brought Tom in a faint back to the Phelpses, he didn't know where or hardly who he was.

So Jim stuck by Tom through everything, but that meant that he got catched and was back in the hut. This time it was a real safe jail; chained up every which way; and a guard dog and men with guns. No way we could've got Jim out of that arrangement.

When Tom waked out of all that doctoring and fainting, he bragged to Aunt Sally and Uncle Silas about what we'd done; now I thought he had really lost his mind. He told them about all those difficulties we'd got up just to make Jim's escape more trouble. When Tom heard that Jim was locked up, he got something furious, saying, "They hain't got no *right* to shut him up! Turn him loose! He ain't no slave! He's as free as any creature that walks this earth!"

"What do you mean, child?" asks Aunt Sally.

"I mean every word I say! And if somebody don't go, I'll go. I've knowed Jim all his life, and so has Tom, there. Old Miss Watson died two months ago, and she was ashamed she ever was going to sell him down the river, and *said* so; and she set him free in her will."

"Then what on earth did *you* want to set him free for, seeing he was already free?" says Uncle Silas.

"Why, I wanted the *adventure* of it!"

That very day Tom's Aunt Polly arrived, and she showed us up to be the liars we are, passing ourselves off as other folk. There warn't no end to the confusion poor Aunt Sally felt. She was one of the mixed-upest looking persons I ever see, except Uncle Silas.

Anyway, after things kind of sorted out to who was who, Aunt Polly she said Tom was right about old Miss Watson setting Jim free in her will; and so, sure enough, Tom Sawyer had gone and took all that trouble and bother to set a free man free!

The first time I catched Tom, private, I asked him what was his idea—what it was he'd planned to do if the escape worked all right and he managed to set a man free that was already free before? And he said, what he had planned in his head, from the start, if we got Jim out all safe, was for us to run him down the river, on the raft, and have adventures plumb to the mouth of the river, and then tell him about his being free, and take him back up home on a steamboat, in style, and pay him for his lost time. But I reckoned it was about as well the way it was.

We had Jim out of the chains in no time, and when Aunt Polly and Uncle Silas and Aunt Sally found out how good he helped the doctor nurse Tom, they made a heap of fuss over him, and fixed him up prime, and

We had Jim out of the chains in no time.

give him all he wanted to eat, and a good time, and nothing to do. And we had him up to Tom's sick-room; and had a talk; and Tom give Jim forty dollars for being prisoner for us so patient, and doing it up so good, and Jim was pleased most to death.

And then Tom he talked along, and says, let's all three slide out of here, one of these nights, and go for howling adventures amongst the Injuns, over in the Territory, for a couple of weeks or two; and I says, all right, that suits me, but I ain't go no money for to buy the outfit, and I reckon I couldn't get none from home, because it's likely Pap's been back before now, and got it all way from Judge Thatcher and drunk it up.

"No, he hain't," Tom says; "it's all there, yet—six thousand dollars and more; and your pap hain't ever been back since."

Jim says, kind of solemn, "He ain't comin' back no mo', Huck."

I says, "Why, Jim?"

"Nemmine why, Huck—but he ain't comin' back no mo'."

But I kept at him; so at last he says, "Doan you 'member de house dat was float'n down de river, en dey wuz a man in dah, kivered up, en I went in en unkivered him, and didn't let you come in? Well, den, you can git yo' money when you wants it; 'cause dat wuz him."

Tom's most well, now, and got his bullet round his neck on a chain, and is always looking at it, and so there ain't nothing more to write about, and I am rotten glad of it, because if I'd a knowed what a trouble it was to make a book I wouldn't a tackled it and ain't agoing to no more. But I reckon I got to light out for the Territory ahead of the rest, because Aunt Sally says she's going to adopt me and civilize me, and I can't stand it. I been there before.

THE END. YOURS TRULY, HUCK FINN